DATE DUE

The Shining Mark

The sequel to
When a Hero Dies

by
Anne Schraff

Perfection Learning Corporation
Logan, Iowa 51546

Cover Illustration: Mark Bischel
Cover Design: Deborah Lea Bell

1 TONY GIBBS STARTED up the front steps to Adams High School and stopped short. Up at the top, a beautiful, dark-skinned woman stood near the double doors, looking around. Her dangling, gold earrings glittered in the Monday morning sun beneath her short, stylish hair. As she put her hand up to shade her eyes, Tony noticed that her long, red nails were well groomed.

But what really struck Tony's eye was the huge diamond ring the woman was wearing. It looked big enough and bright enough to blind anyone who stared at it too long.

Who is she? Tony wondered as he continued up the steps. A new teacher? Then one of the doors opened, and Bruce Campbell emerged from the school. Mr. Campbell was Tony's American Democracy teacher. He smiled at the woman with the diamond ring and spoke to her in a low voice. The woman threw back her head and let loose a throaty laugh. Then she handed the teacher a stack of papers and turned to leave. She passed Tony without looking at him, leaving behind the strong scent of expensive perfume.

Suddenly someone gave Tony a little shove from behind. Tony barely caught himself from tripping on the top step. Turning, he saw Wayman Townes almost right in his face. Wayman was in Tony's class, but Tony didn't consider him a friend.

"Where's your manners, boy?" Wayman said, giving Tony another shove. "Don't you know enough to move out of the way when la-dies pass?"

Tony glared at Wayman. He knew he hadn't been in the woman's way at all. But that was just like Wayman. It seemed to Tony that Wayman spent most of his time giving other people grief.

Before Tony could say anything, Wayman's attention turned to Mr. Campbell, who still stood outside the door.

"Mistuh Campbell, bro," Wayman said. "That was one classy lady you were talking to."

Another classmate, Zenza Dunne, joined Wayman. "Yeah," Zenza put in. "You been keeping secrets from us?"

Mr. Campbell glared at Wayman and Zenza. "Don't be crude, Dunne. Though it's none of your business, the lady happens to be Ms. Brittany Austin—my fiancée. Now, if you'll excuse me, I have a class to prepare for." With that, Mr. Campbell turned and disappeared inside. Wayman and Zenza followed him, still joking around, though in lower voices.

Now it was Andre Calder's turn to arrive. Tony and Andre were pretty good friends. They had a lot in common, including their love of sports. While Andre played football, Tony was the star of the Adams High track team.

Apparently Andre had heard Mr. Campbell's words. "Don't he beat all, that dude Campbell," Andre remarked to Tony. "Head of the social studies department and the youngest teacher at Adams. He's got 'em eating out of his hand. And now he's marrying a lady named Brittany! Man, she belongs on the cover of a magazine— not married to some teacher!"

Tony laughed. "He seems to have it all, don't he?"

"You have a good weekend?" Andre asked.

"It was okay. Didn't see Soroya much—she was busy with family stuff. So she's coming over tonight. We're gonna order a pizza and watch some TV." Thinking about Soroya made Tony smile. It had taken a long time for him and Soroya to really get together. But now she was just about the best part of his life. He couldn't wait till tonight.

When classes were over for the day, Tony went to the school gym. There was no track and field practice that day, so Tony and a few others cleaned up the gym instead. As Tony helped put away the sagging volleyball net, he wondered if the school would ever get the money to buy some new athletic equipment. They needed everything—new balls, new nets, new scoreboards. When Tony was older and supporting himself, he'd sure do what he could to help out his school.

When he finally left for home, it was almost dark. The sky had clouded over, and now it was drizzling. Tony jogged quickly, his powerful leg muscles serving him as well as they did in his many track triumphs. He sped past the grocery store where his beloved old friend Mr. Jefferson once did business. He tried to ignore how the store was now a liquor and adult video business.

Two boys flaunting gang colors yelled something. But Tony sprinted on, his nerves tense. Last month on this street a man had been shot for no reason. A bullet had come from nowhere, leaving the man face down in the asphalt. Nobody knew why. Probably nobody ever would.

But Tony refused to think about that. His mind was on how good life was going for him. He had Mama and his twelve-year-old sister Shauna and track and field and Soroya. And that just about summed up the joyful part of Tony Gibbs' life.

Sometimes Tony thought that life was too good—that maybe his happiness wouldn't last. But he always forced those dark thoughts out of his head.

The apartment building Tony lived in loomed ahead. Mama would still be napping, he knew. She worked hard at the post office sorting mail. Shauna would be doing homework on the kitchen table.

When Soroya came over, the living room would belong to Tony and Soroya. They'd sit on the lumpy sofa, watching TV and enjoying pepperoni pizza.

Tony sprinted up the stairs, two at a time. Inside the apartment, he kicked off his wet shoes. Shauna greeted him, then said, "Michelle called."

"Michelle who?" Tony asked, half smiling.

"You know Michelle who," Shauna said, tossing her head. "Your gorgeous ex-girlfriend, Michelle Calder. When I'm in high school, I'm gonna be beautiful like that girl."

"In a pig's eye," Tony said, laughing. "You ain't got no dark gold topaz eyes like her." He was just teasing his sister. Tony used to admire Michelle's beautiful eyes, but no more.

"Shut your mouth, Tony-baloney," Shauna said, giving Tony a playful punch. "You're such a bad dude. You got a different girlfriend every month!"

"No, I don't. Me and Soroya are real tight," Tony said. "Speaking of Soroya, she's coming over. Should be here any time now." He glanced at the small clock on the kitchen counter.

Suddenly the calm was shattered by a scream and a sharp screech of brakes. The sounds came from the street below.

Tony ran over to the window and peered out. But the rain and the darkness formed a shroud over everything. He squinted his eyes and looked hard. Dimly he could see people running out into the street. Someone hit by a car, Tony thought.

Tony peered closer. He spotted something bright yellow lying in the middle of the street. It was toward this splash of yellow that people were hurrying.

Tony's heart jumped to his throat. Soroya always wore her yellow raincoat when it rained.

"Oh, God," Tony breathed.

"What is it?" Shauna asked, her dark eyes big in her face. She looked like a deer caught in headlights. "What happened?" She grabbed Tony's arm and shook him.

"I don't know," Tony moaned. But in his heart, he did know. As Shauna phoned for an ambulance, sickness and terror spread through Tony's body. This was about the time when Soroya would have been crossing the street, heading for his place. What if it was Soroya—

No, no, no! cried a voice inside Tony's head. It couldn't be. Not Soroya. She couldn't be lying down there in the street with all those people leaning over her.

"Tony?" Mrs. Gibbs had awakened from her nap. Now she stood in her bedroom doorway staring at her son. "Lord in heaven, child, you look like you just seen a ghost."

"Mama," Tony gasped, "somebody down there's been hit by a car—I think it's Soroya..."

"What!" Mrs. Gibbs exclaimed. She ran over to the window. "Why, I can't see a thing in the rain and the dark. What makes you think it's Soroya?"

But Tony was already out the door, stumbling down the stairs like a drunken person. He tried hard to calm himself. Lots of people have yellow raincoats, he thought. That flash of yellow didn't mean anything.

But if it wasn't Soroya, then why was his heart burning with anguish? Why did he feel like he did on that awful day when he learned Mr. Jefferson had been murdered?

Tony pushed his way through the people in the wet street. A man Tony didn't know was holding the motionless person in his arms, shaking his head sadly.

Tony looked down at the unconscious girl, and his legs started to crumble. "Soroya!" Tony sobbed. "Oh, God, no!"

The paramedics and the police arrived then. Tony and the rest of the crowd were forced to move back. Tony stood on the sidewalk, rain dripping off him. He stared at all the commotion with horror.

Yes, that was Soroya in her yellow raincoat. Only now the raincoat was ripped and dirty.

A sharp cry shook Tony out of his thoughts. He looked up. Soroya's mother and father were running in the street toward their daughter.

"That's my baby!" Mrs. Curtis was crying. "My baby!"

Tony watched numbly as the unconscious girl was lifted into the ambulance. Mr. Curtis spoke briefly with a police officer. Then he and his wife climbed into the ambulance with their daughter.

Almost before Tony knew what was happening, the vehicle took off down the street. The sound of the siren stayed in Tony's head long after the ambulance disappeared.

Disjointed memories of Soroya at school that day swam in Tony's brain. Soroya laughing in the hallway. Soroya joking around in the lunchroom. Soroya serious and intent in math class.

Math class. They'd been talking about statistics and life expectancy charts that day. Soroya mentioned some people she knew who'd died very young.

Tony had told her she'd live to be a hundred at least. "I can picture you, girl—a little hundred-year-old grandma in a white, ruffled bonnet," he'd said.

Soroya had laughed at that. Now her laughter echoed and re-echoed in Tony's brain. Tears ran down his cheeks and mixed with the rain. It was like a terrible nightmare. All he wanted was to wake up and say, "Man, oh man, Mama, I had a baaaad dream."

Tony felt a hand slip into his, and he jumped, startled. It was Shauna. He hadn't even noticed her standing next to him.

"She'll be all right," Shauna was saying to him. "I just know it."

Tony shook his head, too choked up to answer.

The police began asking people what they had seen. Dimly, Tony heard the different voices: "Brakes screeching, didn't see no car, though,"... "Car musta took off again without even stopping"... "...Gone before we even realized what happened"... "Hit-and-run, I guess..."

Some witnesses thought they saw a dark car. But others thought the car was light-colored. Nobody got a license number or had a clue as to who the driver was.

One old woman who was questioned lived on the streets. People in the neighborhood called her Lady Greensleeves because she always wore a ragged green coat. But she couldn't give any information either. She just danced around, singing,

"Tell them at the Round Table that the dragon is nigh."

The police officer taking statements shook his head and closed his book. "Not much here," he said.

"She's my girl," Tony told the officer. He had to tell somebody. "She's my girl—the one that was hit."

"Tough break, kid," the officer said.

Tony called Andre, and they drove down to the hospital in Andre's car. Shauna had wanted to come too. But Tony told her to stay home. He didn't know how late he'd be.

"Soroya was coming to see me, Andre," Tony said when they were in the car. His voice was shaking. "To see me!"

"So what, man?" Andre said. "What's that got to do with anything?"

"If she hadn't been coming to see me, she'd be okay. Maybe there's a curse on me, Andre. Maybe people who get close to me die, you know? Like Mr. Jefferson!"

"You're talkin' crazy, man. That psycho killed Mr. Jefferson. Didn't have nothing to do with you. And some fool hit Soroya—wasn't your fault, man. Don't go talkin' crazy."

Andre parked, and they went into the hospital lobby. There was no news yet, so Andre got them both coffee. Tony swallowed the hot liquid in one big gulp. He didn't even notice how it burned his throat.

Tony recalled his friend Mr. Jefferson. He had been like the father Tony hardly ever had. His kindly smile and words of encouragement had cheered Tony on during all those track meets. Then he died. And suddenly there was Soroya cheering Tony on, her big eyes on fire with love and enthusiasm.

And now... now somebody had struck Soroya down. Tony shut his eyes tight. Losing another friend was something he didn't think he could handle.

2 "SHE'LL BE OKAY," Andre said over and over. "You'll see. That Soroya is a strong girl."

The big double doors in the lobby opened, and Andre's sister, Michelle, stood there. She looked oddly small, wrapped in a red raincoat. She ran to Tony and took his big hand in her small one.

"I heard the awful news, Tony," Michelle said in a voice barely above a whisper. "I'm real sorry."

"Yeah," Tony said. He wanted to thank Michelle for coming. It was a real classy thing to do. Especially since Michelle thought Soroya "stole" Tony from her. Michelle didn't seem to remember that she and Tony had never really dated.

But Tony's tongue seemed stuck to the roof of his dry mouth. He couldn't make any words come out.

"Probably it was somebody who'd been drinking," Michelle said. "Some creep too drunk to know he'd hit anybody."

Tony closed his eyes again. A few hot tears pressed through and ran down his cheeks. He kept thinking of one of Soroya's favorite quotes: "It's not how long you live that counts. It's how you make the time you get count."

"There's Soroya's sister now," Andre said.

Tony's eyes flew open. "Denique!" he almost shouted. "How is she?"

Denique Curtis was two years older than Soroya. She attended the junior college. Her usually calm face was now twisted with pain. "She's still unconscious, Tony. They're afraid she's slipped into a coma. They're taking a CAT scan now to see if there's bleeding in the brain. If there is, then they gotta operate to stop the pressure."

"But she's gonna make it," Tony said. "She's gonna be okay, right, Denique?"

Denique's eyes filled with tears. She whispered brokenly, "I don't know, Tony. I just don't know."

Tony turned sharply and headed outside. Andre ran after him, calling, "Hold on, man. I'm driving you home, remember?"

Tony ignored his friend. He sprinted through the double doors into the night. The rain had almost stopped. A fine mist blew sharply against his face.

"Tony!" he heard Michelle shout. "It's four miles to your apartment. That's too far for you to walk—wait!"

"Don't be stupid, man," Andre yelled.

Tony was running so fast now that the buildings lost their shape. It began to rain hard again. The wind whipped his wet shirt around his body. Tony stopped for a minute and banged his clenched fists against a brick wall.

"Why'd I have to ask her over tonight?" he moaned to himself. "Why, why, why!"

He ran on, past walls disfigured by graffiti. The taggers had been busy last night, armed with cans of spray paint. Red and blue and black initials had been scrawled into all available space.

Tony's tears mixed with the rain as his legs moved faster and faster. It was as if he were trying to somehow outrun the night and the terrible event that tore his heart.

When Tony reached his apartment, he stood in the doorway, panting. A puddle of water formed at his feet.

"Tony!" his mother cried. "You're soaking wet! You want to catch your death, child?"

"How is she, Tony?" Shauna asked softly.

"She's bad," Tony said. "Her head is busted, all because she was coming over to visit me!"

"Now, don't go blaming yourself," Mrs. Gibbs said. "Some fool driver is to blame."

Shauna went to Tony and hugged him. "I'll pray real hard, Tony. Reverend Holt said—"

"I don't want to talk about it," Tony snapped. He pulled away from his sister and stalked to his room. He flopped down on his bed and stared at the ceiling. Spiders were busily spinning webs in the corners.

It just wasn't fair. Dark, angry thoughts swarmed Tony's brain. The street was full of worthless people, drug dealers, and gangs. How come Soroya had to get hit? How come somebody beautiful and precious like Soroya had to be the one?

Tony remembered when they studied the assassination of President John F. Kennedy in history class last year. While they watched a movie of the smiling young president, Soroya had brushed away a tear.

" 'Death loves a shining mark,' " she'd said. "That's what an old-time poet wrote. It sure fits President Kennedy's assassination."

Yeah, Tony thought bitterly. Soroya was a shining mark too. Just like Mr. Jefferson had been. But it wasn't fair. Tony felt like pounding the cheap plaster walls of this rotten old apartment until the whole building came tumbling down. But that wouldn't help Soroya.

For the rest of the night Tony tossed and turned, unable to sleep. When morning came, he felt as if a ton of bricks rested on his head. Still, he rose and got ready for school. He had a math test and a paper due in American Democracy. And anyway, Tony figured he was better off at school than going crazy walking the streets.

An early morning phone call from Denique gave Tony little comfort. "She's in a coma," Denique said in a wooden voice. She also informed Tony that Soroya was on a ventilator to help her breathe.

Tony was too upset to eat breakfast. He grabbed his books and headed for school. As he neared Adams High, he caught up with Andre and Michelle.

"Hey, Tony," Andre greeted him. "Any news?"

"No change," Tony said.

"That was a fool thing you did last night, running home, man. Some gang guns could've mistaken you for an enemy in their territory. You're lucky you weren't blown away."

"Yeah," Michelle chimed in. "Being stupid won't help anybody."

"I don't much care what happens to me if Soroya doesn't make it," Tony said, his voice tight.

"Don't say that, Tony," Michelle said softly.

"I'm a jinx," Tony insisted. "People get too close to me and bad things happen to them."

Zenza Dunne was standing nearby. "I hear you, Gibbs," he said. "You're a jinx, all right. With friends like you, who needs enemies? When we run that relay on Saturday, you'll probably brain me with the baton."

"Shut up, Dunne," Andre said.

Tony stared at Zenza, a guy he'd battled with most of his life. Zenza was a bully, always looking for a weakness in somebody. Tony hated having to treat Zenza like a teammate on the track team. But right now he couldn't even work up his usual anger against his enemy.

When Tony entered his American Democracy class, Mr. Campbell wasn't there yet. That was unusual. He always came early so he could fill the board with a lot of material.

"Old Campbell's cuttin' class," Wayman laughed.

Just then there were sharp voices in the hall. A woman snapped, "I'm not one of your stupid little teenagers!"

"Shhh!" Mr. Campbell said in a hushed tone.

"Don't shush me! I will not be lectured!"

"Brittany, I'm late for class," he pleaded.

High heels quickly clicked down the hall, and Mr. Campbell rushed into the room. He looked more flustered than Tony had ever seen him.

"Okay," Mr. Campbell said hurriedly.

"Today we're going to talk about the powers of the presidency."

"He's the boss, right, Mr. Campbell?" Zenza said. "The main man in the country, except maybe with his wife. Then he's just another henpecked dude."

A ripple of laughter flowed through the class. Everyone knew Zenza was referring to Mr. Campbell and his fiancée.

"Cut it out, Dunne," Mr. Campbell snapped. "I'm in no mood for you today!"

Zenza leaned over and whispered to Wayman, "Poor dude. Looks like that Brittany babe's too much for him to handle."

Wayman snickered, then quickly put on a straight face when Mr. Campbell glared at him.

Tony realized he had forgotten his American Democracy paper that was due.

"I left it at home," he told Mr. Campbell after class.

"Great," Mr. Campbell said. "One of my few good students and now you're irresponsible too."

"Mr. Campbell, didn't you hear about Soroya?"

Mr. Campbell frowned. "Soroya Curtis? Yes, I heard she was in some accident. That's too bad. But what does that have to do with—"

"In some accident?" Tony almost yelled. "Is that what you call it when she could be dying, Mr. Campbell?"

The teacher drew back, somewhat alarmed. "Hold on, Gibbs," he said. "I didn't know it was that serious."

"She's in a coma," Tony said. "She may never wake up again!" He turned and hurried out of the classroom. His temper was out of control again. He had thought all of that was behind him after he'd gotten over the grief of losing Mr. Jefferson.

Some writer—maybe it was Hemingway—talked about "grace under pressure." Tony figured he didn't have much of that. He just couldn't hold it together when life got really bad.

Out in the hall, Michelle was waiting for him. "Tony—" she began.

"I don't want to talk now, Michelle," Tony said. "Just leave me alone, okay?"

Michelle gripped Tony's arm. "Listen to me. You're tearing yourself apart over what happened to Soroya. You're blaming yourself when it's not your fault. And you want to know what I think? I think that girl wasn't very good for you anyway."

Tony turned and looked hard into the topaz eyes he'd once so admired. "What? You gone simple? Soroya's the best thing that ever happened to me, Michelle."

"She's one crazy girl," Michelle insisted. "Always talking about death and dying and stuff. She's been bad for you, Tony. She's been dragging you down."

Tony stared at Michelle in disbelief. "Let go of me, Michelle. I don't want to hear any more of this." He tried to shake free of Michelle's grasp.

But Michelle wasn't finished. "Know what I think, Tony? I think she jumped in front of that car on purpose. Think about it. All those gloomy poems old Ms. Applegate was throwing at us all the time. Everybody hated them but Soroya. She loved them. She couldn't get enough of those poems about dying and stuff—"

"Get away from me, Michelle," Tony said grimly.

"Okay, you big fool," Michelle cried.

"But someday you're gonna realize that what I'm saying is the truth. Soroya didn't want to live anymore!"

3 FOR SEVERAL MINUTES after Michelle left, Tony stood there in a state of shock. Surely Michelle couldn't be right. There wasn't anything wrong with Soroya, was there? Had he been too blind to notice that she was crying out for help? Was he so lost in his own happiness that he never noticed her sorrow?

Tony recalled his father, the hazy character who had disappeared when Tony was a small boy. It had come as such a shock to everybody when he vanished without a trace.

Mama had called it a "bolt from the blue." But was it? Maybe no one had noticed the man was slowly sinking under a tide of troubles.

No, Tony decided. Soroya was happy and full of life. A true "shining mark." She would never have jumped in front of a car—never, never. She came from a house full of love and laughter and good, warm parents.

And yet, he did remember how she loved poems like "Crossing the Bar." Those sad, gloomy lines really were her favorites.

Tony had to be sure. After school he jogged over to the Curtis house. Most of the family were down at the hospital, but Denique was home. Looking at her, Tony realized for the first time how much she resembled Soroya.

"Come on in, Tony," Denique said. "I tried to call you. The radiologist finished her tests. At least for now, Soroya won't need to be operated on. About all anyone can do is wait for her to wake up."

"I hope it's soon," Tony said with feeling. He paused, but he couldn't hold the terrible thought to himself any longer. "Denique, I gotta know something. Did Soroya have any problems she was keeping to herself?"

Denique's dark eyes widened. "What do you mean, Tony?"

"It's just that—well, somebody at school is saying she was depressed or something, and maybe—" It was hard to say the awful words. "Maybe Soroya got in front of that car on purpose."

"On purpose?" Denique gasped.

"I don't believe it, but—"

"Oh, Tony, that's the craziest thing I ever heard. Soroya—she's always so happy it gets on our nerves sometimes. Especially since you guys got together."

Denique's eyes welled with tears. "That's why this is so hard. To see her hooked up to that IV machine and the ventilator...to see her so quiet...It's just so unlike Soroya."

Tony reached out and took Denique in his arms, comforting her. She put her head on his shoulder and wept softly. Tony noticed Denique wore the same perfume Soroya wore—faintly sweet, fresh, dewy, like a spring morning.

Tony felt for just a moment that he was holding Soroya, that they'd met for a quick hug in the back of the library. Then grief swept through him like a tidal wave. He wondered if he would ever hold Soroya in his arms again.

Later, Tony walked alone down the street towards home. Denique had settled his doubts about Soroya deliberately running into traffic. He hadn't really believed it in the first place. But Michelle had planted that little doubt in his head.

That was just like Michelle. Just when she and Tony were getting interested in each other, she decided to go out with Zenza Dunne. Then when that turned sour, she was eager to get back with Tony. And when he was no longer interested, she had been hurt and angry.

Tony couldn't imagine how he could ever have liked Michelle in the first place. Sure, she was beautiful, but how far did that go? She was like a book with a pretty cover and nothing inside.

Tony suddenly wondered if Mr. Campbell was in the same boat right now—dazzled by beautiful Brittany Austin, a woman who maybe only had as much quality as Michelle Calder.

But that was unfair. Tony didn't even know Brittany Austin. Who knew, she might be beautiful on the outside and inside. Like Soroya.

Tony stopped in front of the building where Mr. Jefferson's grocery store used to be. His heart ached. If only he could go in there right now and find the man with the mahogany skin and the gentle eyes. Mr. Jefferson would sit Tony down and talk, and somehow Tony would feel better.

But that wasn't to be. Now a young clerk stood behind the counter peddling booze and sleaze. And the absentee owner would never even drive through this neighborhood, much less live here.

Whoever the owner was, he didn't see the results of too much booze and sleaze. He didn't see the empty-eyed alcoholics who stumbled into gutters. He didn't see the drunken kids staggering to cars they might be driving to their own destruction.

Tony stared into the store, his blood beginning to boil. There were rumors that kids could buy liquor in there. Maybe some kids had come in and gotten blind drunk on the booze they got here. Then maybe they'd run down Soroya Curtis.

Tony felt like walking in with a two-by-four and smashing all those rows of bottles. How he'd love to see their powerful contents splashing all over the dirty magazines.

Tony's train of thought was suddenly

broken. He remembered this was the night he visited Edith Haley, the blind lady. With everything that had happened, he'd completely forgotten.

It was Edith Haley who had helped Tony solve the murder of Mr. Jefferson. Tony was really grateful to her for that. So it seemed a very small thing to do to spend a few hours a week reading her favorite books to her.

Mr. Jefferson had been Mrs. Haley's special friend, visiting her and reading to her whenever he could. That had been the highlight of her bleak and mostly joyless week. Tony liked to think he was carrying on in Mr. Jefferson's place. He couldn't fail her, even as bad as he felt now.

Tony crossed the street to the run-down apartment building where Edith Haley lived with her daughter and grandchildren. His strong legs carried him quickly up the stairs to the second floor.

"Oh, Tony," said Mrs. Haley's daughter, Eva, when she saw him. "I didn't think you were coming. Really, you've been so faithful. It just amazes me. I'd think it would be so hard for a boy your age to spend so much time with someone like ... my mother."

"I enjoy it," Tony said. He didn't like Eva much. She never bothered to read to her mother herself. She just tolerated the old lady. Tolerated her and waited for the day when Mrs. Haley would die.

Eva sometimes told Tony how she planned to use the small amount of money her mother would leave her. "A long ocean cruise," she'd say with a tired smile. "I want to be pampered for once in my life."

Tony walked into the living room. Mrs. Haley was there, sitting in a large, over-stuffed chair. As always, her face seemed intelligent and full of life—even with her sightless eyes.

"Tony!" Mrs. Haley said, her face breaking into a smile. "I thought that was you. You have such a nice, deep voice. I swear you're getting to sound just like Hiram Jefferson. He had a fine voice too, didn't he? I always told him that when he got to heaven, they'd let him lead the choir."

"Yeah," Tony replied.

"Tony, you sound unhappy, dear. Is something wrong?" Mrs. Haley asked.

"Well, yeah. It's my girl, Soroya Curtis—you remember, I told you about her. Well, she was hit by a car, and she's in the hospital, hurt real bad." Tony said.

"Oh, my. Oh, dear Lord!" Mrs. Haley reached out and grasped Tony's hands, giving them a squeeze. Even though she was blind, she always managed to find Tony's hands. "Who was driving the car?"

"Hit-and-run," Tony replied.

"Oh, that is so wicked. Somebody not even stopping to see if they could help." There was real grief in Mrs. Haley's voice. Tony appreciated that. Mrs. Haley didn't even know Soroya. Yet she really seemed to care about her.

Tony and Mrs. Haley spent the whole two hours talking. When it was time to go, Tony said, "I haven't even read to you. You wanted to hear more of *The House of the Seven Gables.*"

"Oh, it was more important to talk, Tony. I feel like you're almost family. And when there's a tragedy, why, the family has to pull together," Mrs. Haley said.

Tony stooped and kissed Mrs. Haley good night. Then he hurried out into the darkness. He still felt terrible about Soroya. But talking about it with someone who cared helped—just a little—to ease the pain.

4 THERE WAS A new track and field coach at Adams this year. His name was Lew Shaw. He was a Native American from Oregon, part of a group now called Warm Springs Indians.

Lew Shaw had left the reservation he was born on to get a college degree in P.E. He'd been a splendid runner himself, with a real shot at the Olympics. Then he lost part of his foot while serving in the Marines.

Now Lew Shaw was determined to bring the championship trophy to the Adams Bobcats track team. He made no secret of seeing Tony Gibbs as the key to his dream.

"Ready for the big relay race on Saturday, Gibbs?" he asked Tony at Wednesday morning's practice.

"No, Coach, I got personal problems," Tony said, stifling a yawn. He'd been awake most of the night before, worrying about Soroya.

"Girl trouble?"

"My girl—Soroya—she's been in a coma since Monday night and might not make it. Hit-and-run accident," Tony explained. He expected some sympathy, but the coach frowned instead.

"I feel for you, kid, but that's no excuse for slacking off on the team. Is it gonna help your girl if you don't do your best for yourself and the team? How are you gonna feel when she gets well and wants to see the team trophy? You're gonna have to say, 'Honey, I blew it 'cause I was moping around for you.' What's she gonna think then?"

Tony glared at the coach. He felt Lew Shaw just wanted the glory for himself. The coach didn't care about Tony or Soroya or anybody else. He just aimed to be the first rookie coach who brought a championship trophy to Adams.

"Running's not important to me just now, man," Tony said.

"Is that right? Well, excuse me, Gibbs, but I figured you were a man. I didn't figure you for a crybaby kid. And what about shooting for the Olympics? That's all I ever hear you talk about. This kind of attitude sure isn't going to get you there."

"Look, I don't need this," Tony snapped.

"You want to know what you need, Gibbs? You need to be a Warm Springs Indian kid whose parents died before he was eleven. A kid who didn't know what love was. A kid who figured his trick to glory was running for the Olympic gold—until he got his foot blown off."

Tony sighed. It was Lew Shaw's own story. The coach had told Tony they'd said around the reservation that Shaw would be the new Jim Thorpe. Maybe even the greatest American athlete of all time.

"Get out there and run, Gibbs," the coach barked. "You got the gift—use it!"

Tony began doing laps, finding the old speed returning to his legs. He remembered how Mr. Jefferson would sit there and cheer him on. Soroya did the same thing. But now there was nobody but himself. He was running alone—all alone.

Tony knew that he couldn't win any race if Soroya was still in a coma. Lew Shaw could shame him into practicing. But the coach couldn't give him the heart to win.

At lunchtime that day, Michelle sat down at Tony and Andre's table.

"Andre, I need your car tonight, okay?" Michelle said.

"Use Mama's car," Andre answered. He owned an old convertible he was restoring. He didn't want anybody else driving it.

"You know I can't drive Mama's car for two weeks," Michelle said. "I need to borrow your car—please!"

"You used Mama's car the other night and you busted a headlight," Andre said. "You think I'm gonna trust you with my wheels?"

"I had a tiny little stupid accident," Michelle said. "And I even paid Mama for the repair already. Andre, you're so selfish that I hate you sometimes. You're never there for me—never, ever!"

Andre sighed and looked at Tony, who was trying to read a story for English. Tony'd read the same story—or tried to— three times. And still he didn't understand a word. His mind was far away, over there in the hospital with a girl who couldn't wake up.

"Tony," Andre said, "Michelle drove

Mama's car Monday night and she busted a headlight. Now she has the nerve to ask for my car."

Tony looked up. "Monday night? That's the night Soroya got—"

"Yeah," Michelle said. "What a crummy night that was. Musta been a full moon or something. I bust a stupid headlight on a tree and Soroya gets hit. A real bad-luck night."

Tony stared at Michelle in disbelief. Was she really so callous as to be comparing her little accident with Soroya's tragedy? Michelle was so self-centered, so unfeeling.

Suddenly Tony's eyes narrowed. He began to think the unthinkable. Michelle was such a lousy driver. Maybe she was coming down Central Avenue in the dark as she often did, just to spy on Tony. Could she have struck Soroya, busted the headlight, then sped off in a panic?

"Where did you hit that tree, Michelle?" Tony asked slowly. "Where do you find a tree in this neighborhood?"

Michelle stared at Tony. "I drove over to a mall. I do get out of this crummy neighborhood once in a while, you know. Tony, why are you looking at me like that? What's the matter?"

"When a car hits a person, sometimes there's not much damage," Tony said. "A dent, maybe. Or... a busted headlight?"

"I'm hearing it, but I don't believe it," Andre declared. "Just what are you trying to say, man?"

"Michelle can't drive worth spit," Tony snapped. "She's all the time cruising down Central and lookin' up at my window to see what she can see. Maybe she was doing that Monday night when Soroya crossed the street. Maybe it was Michelle who hit her!"

"You gonna let him say stuff like that to me, Andre?" Michelle demanded in a shrill voice. "What kind of a brother are you?"

"Tony," Andre said, "calm down. Think about it. There was no broken glass at the scene of the accident. Now don't you think there would have been broken glass on the street if Michelle hit Soroya?"

Tony wasn't convinced. "Michelle," he said, "you came up with that creepy story about Soroya jumping in front of the car.

Maybe you were just trying to cover for yourself!"

"Tony Gibbs, how dare you accuse me of doing such a thing!" Michelle cried. "It just makes me sick that I ever liked you at all. I never want to speak to you again!" With that, the angry girl stomped out of the lunchroom.

"Tony, Michelle would freak if she ever hit somebody," Andre said. "Man, you must really be out of your mind not to know that. Michelle wouldn't have the guts to do something like that and then playact about it."

"It's just weird that she busts up the front end of your mama's car the night Soroya was hit," Tony insisted. He looked at the clock on the wall. Then he picked up his books and headed for his next class.

He didn't really think Michelle hit Soroya, but he wasn't sure. All he was sure of was that the doctors were saying Soroya wasn't waking up like she should be.

In American Democracy class, Mr. Campbell didn't seem himself again. He kept making stupid mistakes. "We've been discussing impeachment as a way of accusing the president of a wrongdoing," he said. "Who can tell me the name of the first president to face impeachment proceedings?"

Wei-Jing raised his hand. "Andrew Johnson," he said.

"No," Mr. Campbell said. "Andrew Jackson."

Tony wasn't exactly a whiz in history. But even he knew it was Johnson and not Jackson who was impeached. "Mr. Campbell," he called out. "Wei-Jing is right. It was Johnson who came after Lincoln, so he must have been the one."

Mr. Campbell blinked and then frowned. He always knew his stuff, and that was one of the reasons he kept good discipline. Everybody respected the fact that he was one smart man. Now he seemed to be losing it. It was a scary thing to watch.

Tony glanced out the window. Out in the faculty parking lot, perched on the fender of Mr. Campbell's car, was Brittany Austin. She was impatiently drumming her fingers on her leather purse. It was obvious she was waiting for Mr. Campbell to be done teaching so they could go somewhere. Maybe Mr. Campbell knew it and that's why he couldn't concentrate.

"Yes, Wei-Jing, of course it was Johnson." Mr. Campbell produced a sick smile. "I must have lost my train of thought."

After class, Tony grabbed his books from his locker and headed outside. He joined a group of students who were walking past the faculty parking lot. Hearing sharp voices, Tony looked toward Mr. Campbell's car. Just as he thought, Ms. Austin and Mr. Campbell were arguing again.

Wayman Townes laughed. "Poor old Campbell," he said. "That baaaad woman is turning him into one crazy dude. That's why, Zenza my man, I intend to play the field. No getting tied down by no female. No la-dy is making me dance to her tune—no way, no how."

Tony overheard part of the heated conversation between Mr. Campbell and Ms. Austin. "You didn't tell me you had sixth period today!" Ms. Austin said, fuming. "It's too hot to sit and fry for an hour while you teach those punks. Not to mention the kind of neighborhood this is. Do you know what could happen to someone like me, out here all alone?"

"What's gotten into you, Brittany? You're so unreasonable," Mr. Campbell said in a lower, but still audible tone.

"Let's go, for God's sake! I'm hot, sweaty, and tired." Brittany got into the car and slammed the door.

Andre whistled. "And he's gonna marry her? You talk about love bein' blind. In his case it's blind and stupid."

Tony didn't say anything. He just hoped he and Soroya would never act like that with each other.

"Tony," said Michelle, coming up to him, "I forgive you if you forgive me— or whatever."

Tony avoided looking at her. "Nothing to forgive," he muttered.

Michelle slipped her soft hand under Tony's arm. "It's just that I care about you so much."

Tony closed his eyes. There was a time he had wanted to hear such words from Michelle. But no more.

"Don't be mad at me, Tony," Michelle

pleaded.

"I'm not," he said. "I just can't think of anything but Soroya lying there in that hospital."

"Remember last year at cheerleader tryouts how you sat there and rooted for me, Tony?" Michelle persisted. "I made a big mistake going with that fool Zenza. But now I know what's good."

"Just leave me alone, Michelle, okay?" Tony said. He turned away from her and bumped into Wayman Townes.

"Heyyy, Tony," Wayman said. "I think I've solved the mystery of ol' Soroya's hit-and-run."

Tony's eyes narrowed, and he demanded, "What're you talking about? You know who hit her?"

"I got sources, know what I mean?" Wayman said. "Only they got a price, my man. Hear what I'm sayin'?"

Tony felt the blood rush to his head as he grabbed Wayman's shirt. "I'll bust your head if you don't tell me!" he roared.

5 AT THAT MOMENT, Ms. Applegate came storming up to Tony and Wayman. She was a stout, dark-skinned teacher who seemed afraid of nothing. "Tony Gibbs!" she cried. "I'm ashamed of you. How dare you threaten another student? I think you'd better see the principal!"

Tony glared at Wayman. Then he turned and followed Ms. Applegate into the school building.

In the principal's office, Lorraine Cheng sat at her desk with her fingers inter-locked. She looked at Tony for a few moments. Then she remarked, "You've been an excellent student, Tony. Fighting is unlike you. What's wrong?"

"I'm sorry, Ms. Cheng. You know what happened to Soroya, don't you?"

"Of course," Ms. Cheng replied. She sounded sympathetic.

"Well, Townes said he knows who hit her and he wanted money to tell."

Anger flashed in Ms. Cheng's eyes. "Well, we'll just see about that. You come with me."

Wayman was shooting baskets with Zenza when Ms. Cheng and Tony approached. "Wayman, what's this I hear about you knowing who struck Soroya?" Ms. Cheng asked.

"I don't know what fool you been talking to, Ms. Cheng," Wayman said. He shot an evil look at Tony.

"Not some fool, Wayman," said Ms. Cheng. "Now you listen to me. Hit-and-run is a serious crime. You could get into big trouble by hiding information." The principal's voice was like ice. She seemed more than a match for six-foot tall Wayman Townes—all five-feet-two of her.

"Heyy...look...I was just talking about speculation, Ms. Cheng. Yeah, speculation..."

"So you were trying to extort money from Tony Gibbs when you really had no information," Ms. Cheng said.

"Uh...no, not exactly," Wayman mumbled.

Ms. Cheng sighed and shook her head.

She walked back inside, followed by Tony.

"I believe Wayman doesn't know any more than you or I," Ms. Cheng declared back in her office. "He saw a chance to pick up some easy money. But I'm sure he knows nothing about the accident."

Tony looked down for a moment. He knew Ms. Cheng was right. And he was ashamed of blowing up. It seemed his explosive temper would never settle down. When he got mad, it was like he turned into dynamite. He exploded whenever anybody lit a match.

"Uh, I'm sorry, Ms. Cheng," he told the principal. "It's just that I'm so worried about Soroya. It burns me that whoever did it got clean away."

"I'm sure the police will find the driver," Ms. Cheng said.

"They got drive-by shootings, gangs, robberies, murders," Tony said glumly. "What time they got for a hit-and-run?"

When Tony headed home, Wayman and Zenza were still shooting baskets.

"Someday you gonna be a whipped dog, Gibbs," Wayman yelled. "And when you look up with a bloodied face, it's me you're gonna see."

"Zenza already tried to whip me, Wayman Townes," Tony shot back. "And you ain't half what he is."

Tony loped toward home. The characters were coming out now. The petty criminals. The ones who did crack. The ones who'd sunk their lives into a pit of drugs or booze.

Tony glanced at the faces—the hard, often mean faces. He remembered some of them when they were little kids. There was a time when he'd even played with them on these very streets.

There was Rafe—a good kid once. When Tony gashed his knee, Rafe had patched it up. That seemed like ancient history now. As Tony passed, Rafe spat out an insult. It was now part of Rafe's way of life to hate boys like Tony.

Then there was Kiwane. At one time he'd been on the track team with Tony. Now he only ran from the police.

Tony kept clear of guys like Rafe and Kiwane. They stood for a world of hatred and dead ends—funerals at an early age.

Soon Tony turned onto his own street. The woman called Lady Greensleeves was sitting on the curb. Seeing Tony, she stood up and called out to him, "She was a witch!"

Tony turned and looked at the woman. Bright eyes peered back at him through graying hair, which drifted like cobwebs over her haggard face.

"Ma'am?" he asked.

"She was a witch. A devil. I asked her for a few coins. Pretty miss, pretty miss, I says to her. I have need of a cup of tea." A frown twisted the old woman's face, as if she'd tasted something bitter.

"But she, she says to me, 'You make me sick, old hag. You should be wiped off the face of the earth.' "

The old woman suddenly winked. "And I, I say, the world is coming to an end. Hahahahaha! It is being dragged into the ocean by the powers of darkness." The woman did an impromptu little dance, lifting her dark skirt to reveal bony, white-stockinged legs.

Tony felt sorry for the woman. She was one of the many mentally ill people with no one to care for them. Tony reached into his pocket for a dollar. He put it in the woman's grimy hand.

"Bless you, Prince Valiant," said Lady Greensleeves. She gave a little curtsy. "Tell them at the Round Table that you have done well. Tell the fair Aleta that the shiny blue dragon shall burn in the infernal sea…slimy, shiny, awful, awful…"

Tony hurried on, but her wavy voice followed him. "Tell Aleta not to cry. There'll be joy in the bye and bye."

Tony sprinted up the stairs to his apartment. Inside, he found his mother in a bad mood.

"It's about time you got home," his mother said to him in a grumpy voice. "Lot of chores waitin' to get done. You get yourself out here and take the garbage down. Lord, half the time I forget I even have a son for the little time you're home."

On his way to get the garbage, Tony stopped and kissed his mother on the cheek. "Love you, Mama," he said.

Mrs. Gibbs' frown faded. She gave her son a tired smile. "You're a good boy, Tony," she said, patting his arm.

Tony gathered the garbage and carried it downstairs to the alley. It was dark now. A sliver of moon stood in the sky like a raised sword.

Shauna followed Tony down with a bag he'd missed. "Toss this too, Tony. Uh...hear anything about Soroya?"

"I called Denique from school. No change," Tony said. "They still won't let me in to see her. Family only, the doctor says."

"She's gonna get better, Tony. I feel it in my bones."

"Thanks," Tony said, mussing his little sister's hair. "Hey, you read the comics, don't you?"

"Sometimes. The funny ones," Shauna replied.

"How about Prince Valiant?"

"That's an old one. I got a book where they show old comics. He was super fine," Shauna said.

"Who was Aleta?"

"She was Prince Valiant's girlfriend," said Shauna. "Why?"

"Oh, ol' Lady Greensleeves down on the street kept raving about Prince Valiant," Tony said. "And Aleta and dragons."

"Lady Greensleeves?" Shauna repeated. "She always called Soroya 'Aleta' 'cause Soroya was always slipping her doughnuts and sandwiches. Soroya would laugh, 'cause Aleta in the comics is white and Soroya's black."

Tony forced a garbage pail lid down. "Soroya never told me that," he remarked. In his mind, he turned over what the woman had been raving about.

Aleta not to cry...shiny blue dragon. Suddenly Tony grew cold. He ran upstairs and shouted, "Mama, I'll be back. I gotta check on something." Without waiting for an answer, he raced back down the steps.

Tony recalled that Lady Greensleeves had been there on the street when the hit-and-run driver had struck "Aleta." He remembered she'd said something about a dragon. He had paid no attention to it then. But now she mentioned a "shiny blue dragon."

Tony felt a little dizzy. He knew it was unlikely. But could "shiny blue dragon" refer to the car that hit Soroya?

Tony looked up and down the street, trying to find Lady Greensleeves among the panhandlers and drunks. But she was nowhere in sight. Apparently she had gone somewhere to spend her dollar.

When she left like that, Tony knew, she usually didn't reappear until morning.

Disappointed, Tony went back home. It probably doesn't mean anything anyway, he thought. Probably just the ravings of her poor, sick mind. It was a measure of his desperation that he was grasping at such weak straws.

Later that evening, Tony and Shauna ate macaroni and cheese and cleaned up the dishes. Mrs. Gibbs had already gone to bed. Tony wished for the thousandth time that his mother wasn't so tired all the time.

At eight o'clock the doorbell rang. It was Michelle Calder. She was the last person Tony wanted to see at the moment. Unwillingly he let her into the apartment.

"I know I didn't tell you I was coming over," Michelle said. "But I'm just so worried about you, Tony."

Tony didn't say anything.

"You and me and Andre go back a long time," Michelle went on. She settled herself on the lumpy sofa as if she planned to stay a while. "That's gotta mean something."

"Yeah, sure, we're friends," Tony muttered.

"Tony," Michelle said, "what're you gonna do if Soroya doesn't get better?"

"Don't say that," he said.

"I've got to say it," said Michelle. "Somebody's got to make you face reality. Sometimes they stay in a coma like that for years. You gonna just stop living while she lays there like Sleeping Beauty or something?"

"She's gonna be okay," Tony almost shouted. "She's gonna be fine, like she was before." Tears filled Tony's eyes, blinding him. "She's gonna be laughing and joking and making plans, just like always. Now stop talking like that. I don't want to hear no more!"

6 MICHELLE LISTENED TO Tony's outburst with wide eyes. "Maybe I should go," she said finally. "You're obviously in no mood for visitors."

Tony made no move to stop her as she went toward the door. "I'll see you at school," Michelle said.

"Yeah," Tony muttered.

In bed that night, Tony lay awake for hours, thinking. Just before dawn, he threw on his clothes with fierce determination. The more he thought about Lady Greensleeves, the more he had to see her. He had to draw some sense out of what she was saying.

Tony hurried out into the darkness. He jogged up one street and down another, up one alley and down another. But he couldn't find the woman.

It wasn't unusual for the sick ones to vanish every now and then. You'd wonder if they'd finally died, if the streets had claimed their poor, frail lives. But then they'd reappear, defying the odds to continue their fragile lives.

Tony finally went home to get ready for school. He'd search for Lady Greensleeves again after his last class.

Tony arrived at school earlier than usual. When he went into the American Democracy classroom, Mr. Campbell was already there. He was proudly showing Brittany Austin the new maps he'd cajoled from the school. "Look, my world history students will be able to see how the world really looks since the changes in Europe and Asia."

Ms. Austin seemed unimpressed. She glanced at her diamond-studded watch and hurried from the classroom.

"Good morning, Tony," Mr. Campbell said. He seemed in a cheerful mood. "How's Soroya?"

"She isn't any better yet," Tony said.

"Well, I'm sorry to hear that, but these things take time. No news is good news, I guess."

Tony began telling Mr. Campbell about Lady Greensleeves. "She maybe saw the car that hit Soroya. I'm gonna try to see her this afternoon and find out if she really did see some—"

Tony paused when he saw a movement at the door. Brittany Austin stood there with her hands on her hips, staring at Tony. When he stopped speaking, she turned her attention to Mr. Campbell.

"My keys!" she snapped impatiently. "You've got my keys!"

Mr. Campbell tossed her the keys with an apology. He smiled weakly at his fiancée, who made no move to leave. "This is Tony Gibbs, one of my best students," Mr. Campbell told her. "His girlfriend was seriously injured by a hit-and-run driver. Now he thinks he may have a clue. A homeless woman they call Lady Greensleeves may have seen the culprit."

Brittany Austin stared at Tony as if he were a creature from outer space. Then she said, "I've got to go." She turned down the hall and headed out of the building. Her high heels sounded like machine-gun fire on the hard floors.

Mr. Campbell looked sheepish as he turned to Tony and Andre, who had just arrived. "You must forgive Ms. Austin for not seeming to be interested. She doesn't mean to be rude. But she really doesn't like being in this end of town at all.

"People like Lady Greensleeves frighten her," Mr. Campbell went on. "Ms. Austin was rather sheltered as she was growing up. She'd never had to deal with the…uh…seamier side of life."

"Poor Ms. Austin," Andre said mockingly. "It's a real shame she's got to see how the rest of us live."

Mr. Campbell's expression darkened. "Don't take that attitude, Andre. There's nothing wrong with Ms. Austin wanting to live in a better neighborhood. I can't say that I blame her. This is often a scary place to be. Just because we were born African-American doesn't mean we can't be successful. I make no apology whatever for wanting the very best from life I can get. And Ms. Austin shares that desire."

"How come the good life can't be around here?" Tony asked. "Lots of good people live here."

"Give me a break, Tony," Mr. Campbell said in exasperation. "The graffiti, the garbage, the brown lawns, the gangs—this is a horrible place."

"So why you teaching in a 'horrible place' like this, Mr. Campbell?" Andre asked. His voice dripped with sarcasm.

Mr. Campbell smiled. "Well, I have my idealism too—don't sell me short. I felt it was more or less my duty to spend a few years teaching in a disadvantaged area. There's always the hope that I'll make a difference in one or two lives. I don't mind saying it's a great feeling to be a change agent in a young person's life.

"Like with you, Tony," Mr. Campbell continued. "You'll probably go places. Maybe someday you'll look back and think that a certain social studies teacher helped you get there."

"If I get anywhere, it'll be in this neighborhood," Tony said. "I'm not running away. I'm gonna make things happen right here."

"Well, I admire your courage," Mr. Campbell said. "But I'll not be back here at Adams next year. Ms. Austin's father owns a large computer company. They're developing some exciting software. I'll be in charge."

"You'll be making big bucks, eh, Mr. Campbell?" Tony said. "No more scraping along on a teacher's pay."

"Spare me that tone of voice, Tony." Mr. Campbell said. "Do you know what's one of the biggest things that keeps our people from getting ahead? It's the very attitude you're expressing right now. You and others like you resent those of us who make good lives for ourselves. You think it's somehow admirable to sit in this ugly place and dodge gang bullets. Or watch fools sticking needles in their arms. Or stand in the grocery line behind a welfare mother with five kids."

"My mom's not on welfare," Tony snapped. "Never was, never will be."

"Mine neither," put in Andre. "Both my parents work like dogs for a living."

The bell rang then. Tony got in his seat and tried to concentrate on school. But his mind kept wandering to what Lady Greensleeves had said.

Shiny blue dragon. It was as if the words were glued inside Tony's head. He tried to think of the people he knew who had a blue car. He realized he hardly knew anyone with any car at all, much less a blue one.

Tony was a little relieved at this. He didn't want the hit-and-run driver to be someone he knew.

Later, at the soft drink machine, Tony told Andre and some other kids about Lady Greensleeves. "I'm really wanting to find her. I think maybe she saw the car that hit Soroya."

"That old bat wouldn't remember nothin'," Zenza said. "She's cra-zy. One time me and Wayman went upstairs and pelted her with peanuts. She thought it was hailing. It was like ninety degrees out—really sunny and hot. And she was dancin' around and hollerin', 'It's hailing, it's hailing.' "

"You shouldn't brag about doing such mean things, Zenza," a girl said.

"Making a little fun of a crazy old witch?" Wayman said. "There ain't no harm in that."

Another girl turned to Tony and asked, "How's Soroya? She any better?"

"I'm going over to the hospital after school. Mrs. Curtis said it's finally okay for me to go in and see Soroya," Tony said. "The family's been talking to her, trying to get her to wake up. Nurses too. They keep on saying stuff like 'Who are you?' 'What's your name?' They think that maybe talking to her will pull her back from where she is."

"Maybe you ought to kiss her. That'd wake her up, like old Sleeping Beauty," Wayman said. Then he laughed. "Only if somebody ugly like you kissed her, she'd prob'ly up and die right then and there."

"You want a split lip, Townes?" Tony shot back.

Michelle had been standing nearby, and now she moved in closer. "What she's in is a vegetative state," she said. "My aunt's a nurse. She says they stay like that for months and years and they got to go to a nursing home. There's a young guy in the nursing home where my aunt works. He's been out of it for five years. He's good as dead. But they keep him going with tubes and stuff," Michelle said.

Tony tried to ignore Michelle. But her words cut through his heart like sharp knives. Images floated before him of

Soroya in some nursing home for the rest of her life. He felt a fresh hatred for the driver who'd run her down. He swore to find Lady Greensleeves if it took all night.

* * *

After school, Tony met Shauna at the bus stop. Together they rode to the hospital. Tony felt numb and shaky as he walked into the lobby. He was glad Shauna had come with him. Having her along made it somehow better. Lots of times his little sister seemed like twelve going on thirty.

"What room's she in?" Shauna asked softly.

"Third floor—312," Tony replied. His mouth was dry, and he felt his heart thumping against his chest. Until now only family had been allowed to see Soroya. So she was at least a little better.

Tony tried to steel himself for how she'd look. He dreaded the moment when he would walk into her room. Seeing her connected to those wires and tubes would make her terrible condition all the more real.

Tony and Shauna rode up on the elevator with a pair of nurses who chatted merrily about their boyfriends. It always amazed Tony that people who worked with the sick and injured were still able to lead happy lives.

Tony felt his sister's hand slip into his. "Pray, Tony," she whispered. "It'll make it easier."

Tony gave Shauna a little smile and squeezed her hand. Sometimes he figured Shauna would become a preacher. He could just see her standing in the front of the church, making a joyful noise fit to break anyone's heart. She'd stand there swaying, her slender body all wrapped in a black preacher's dress with a bright kente cloth over her shoulder. Usually thinking of that made Tony smile. Now nothing could.

Room 312 wasn't far from the elevator. Tony stopped at the door and took a deep breath. Bracing himself, he tightened his hold on Shauna's hand and stepped in.

7 MRS. CURTIS SAT at Soroya's bedside. Tony knew she was there most of the time, just going home to snatch a little rest. Those times Mr. Curtis or one of the Curtis kids took her place at Soroya's bedside.

"Come on in, Tony, Shauna," Mrs. Curtis said. She was a very pretty woman, but now her face looked haggard. It seemed like she'd aged ten years in the last few days. Soroya was her youngest child, her baby. Tony had heard that mothers feel special about their last child.

Tony looked down at Soroya and saw an ugly, dark bruise on her cheek. She was hooked to an IV machine, but the ventilator wasn't needed anymore. The doctors said there wasn't any bleeding in her brain, and that was a hopeful sign.

"She's breathing on her own," Mrs. Curtis said. "See?"

"Praise God," Shauna said, just like a preacher would.

"But she won't wake up," Mrs. Curtis said. "I talk to her all the time. I keep telling her I love her and we all love her. I tell her what's been happening. But she just won't wake up."

Tony leaned close to Soroya and whispered, "Baby...talk to me. It's Tony. Love ya, Soroya. Hey, remember the junior picnic, baby? That's when we realized how much we meant to each other. Remember? Soroya?

"Come on, baby—wake up," Tony urged. "Remember when I gave you my junior ring, baby? You made it shine like it never shone before when you put it on your finger. Please, Soroya, open your eyes!"

Soroya made no sign of recognition. Tony looked up at Mrs. Curtis, who was dabbing at tears.

"It's like she's somewhere far away where we can't touch her," Mrs. Curtis said.

"What does the doctor say?" Tony asked.

"He says not to give up hope. He told me to watch for her to move her arms and legs. That's the first sign that they're coming out of it. But she's so still, so very still," Mrs. Curtis said.

"Baby," Tony said, leaning close to Soroya again. "Come on...I love you so much. Don't be hiding from me, baby."

Shauna stepped close to Soroya and softly began singing a hymn.

" 'Precious Lord...you're my shepherd, precious Lord, heeeear my cry, precious Lord, take my hand, leeeead me onnnnnn, hearrrrrr my cry...' "

But nothing would rouse Soroya. She lay there like a statue. Tony bent down to kiss her, then straightened up. He'd been told he could only stay for a few minutes.

"I'll be back every chance I get, Mrs. Curtis," he promised. "Nothing's gonna keep me away."

"She's gonna be okay," Shauna said. "I know it."

Tony and Shauna rode back down on the elevator together.

"Think the doctor is telling Mrs. Curtis the truth? That there's a lotta hope and all?" Tony asked.

"Oh, yeah," Shauna replied. "He's a good doctor. I talked to Denique and she told me all about him. He's from India, and he's brilliant—a real specialist in brain injuries."

"What if she wakes up and...you know, she's different?" Tony asked.

"Like how?"

"Like...you know, she's so smart and everything. What if she's got brain damage? I read where a head injury can do that."

"It won't be like that," Shauna said firmly. "Anyway, we'll still love her. We'll always love her. Tony, God's not gonna let anything happen that we can't handle, you know?"

Tony turned sharply and looked at his little sister. "Where'd you get such faith, Shauna? 'Cause I sure don't have it."

Shauna smiled, and it shocked Tony how beautiful she was getting. He was so used to the cute little girl with braids. This lovely girl with the curly hair and the big, soft eyes surprised him.

"Tony," Shauna said, "you got too much mad in you for faith to get in. You're like a big old steam engine huffin' and puffin'. You just won't let the love and forgiveness come into your heart. See, the faith is gonna come right along then."

"Love and forgiveness for the creep who did that to Soroya?" Tony demanded.

"Just let it go, Tony," Shauna said. "Hating somebody is like holding a stick that's on fire in your hand. Unless you let it go, it'll end up burning you too."

Tony just shook his head. He couldn't let it go. Not yet. After he saw Shauna home, he went in search of Lady Greensleeves. Maybe it was a wild-goose chase. But it was all he had to go on.

Lady Greensleeves had a routine every afternoon. First she searched the dumpsters, looking for fruits. Then she visited the Mexican restaurant where they'd let her have tortillas for nothing. Finally she stopped at the diner where they'd give her coffee. Tony went to all those places. But the people he talked to hadn't seen her that day.

"She never misses her tortilla, man," said Rico at the Mexican restaurant. He shook his head. "She's gotta be sick or something."

Often when Lady Greensleeves finished her rounds, she'd find an alleyway to sleep in. Usually she chose one behind a grocery store. She didn't like to sleep behind places that sold liquor. She was scared of being attacked by drunken, violent men in the middle of the night. But when Tony checked behind her regular grocery store, she wasn't there.

A flutter of wings over Tony's head reminded him of Reggie Dunne, Zenza's little brother. Tony and Reggie had been friends ever since Tony stopped Zenza from pushing Reggie around.

Maybe—just maybe—Reggie, up there with his pigeons, had seen something of Lady Greensleeves. He had a vantage point of the whole neighborhood from his loft.

Tony went up the stairs to the roof of the apartment building where Reggie kept his pigeons. There was Reggie as usual, feeding his birds.

"Hey, my man!" Tony shouted.

Reggie turned, grinning. "Hey, Tony!"

"How's the pigeons, Reggie?"

"Pretty good. Sonni Ali and Sonni Baru showing real fine. And I got some new tumblers."

"Great. Listen, Reggie, do you think you can help me out? I want to talk to this lady they call Lady Greensleeves. Now she's disappeared on me," Tony said.

Reggie gave Tony a funny look. "It's weird you asking about her," Reggie remarked. "She's history, man."

Tony turned cold. "What's that supposed to mean?"

"I got outta school early today," Reggie explained. "Came up here around noon. Wasn't here very long when some dude comes up the street in a dark red Caddy. Was driving real slow. Then he stops and hollers for Lady Greensleeves. I could hear him all the way up here.

"Well, she's scoutin' for food in the dumpster like she always does. She comes over to the Caddy and this guy talks to her some. Well, whatever he says makes her get in the Caddy and away they go."

Hair bristled on Tony's neck. "You ever see that Cadillac before, Reggie?" Tony asked.

"No way, man. Not in this neighborhood. We got lots of Caddies, but they're old junkers. This Caddy had chrome wheels. And I could see that dark red leather inside—it was cool. That's the kinda machine I'm gonna own when I grow up," Reggie declared.

"Did you see the driver?" Tony asked.

"Yeah, some Asian guy," Reggie said. "I think he was a chauffeur dude—had some kind of uniform on. Lady Greensleeves seemed real happy to get in. She was laughing in that crazy kinda way she has."

Tony went back downstairs, thinking hard. He'd been sure he was on to something with Lady Greensleeves. And now a fancy car had picked her up and spirited her away. She never took a bath. Most rich people wouldn't want the likes of her sitting on their fine leather seats. No, it had to have something to do with the hit-and-run. But why had they waited until today to come after her?

Suddenly Tony let out an exclamation. He recalled what he'd done that morning at school. He'd blabbed his thoughts about the "shiny blue dragon" to anybody who'd listen.

Reggie said the Caddy picked Lady Greensleeves up a little after noon to take her away. So between nine and twelve, somebody decided to remove Lady

Greensleeves from the neighborhood.

Tony tried to remember everybody he told. Who among them could afford to hire a driver and a Caddy to take Lady Greensleeves away?

Tony had another thought. Maybe someone he'd told had told somebody else. And maybe that somebody else knew the hit-and-run driver or was the hit-and-run driver.

One thing was certain. No one in this neighborhood had nearly enough money to hire someone to spirit away Lady Greensleeves.

Maybe whoever hit Soroya was dealing crack. But if that were the case, the person probably would have killed Lady Greensleeves on the spot. No, it had to be somebody with money, but not a criminal type.

Tony had the sinking feeling that he'd never see Lady Greensleeves again. He bet she'd been given a bus ticket to another city. If so, she'd take whatever secrets she had with her. And she'd soon forget all about little Aleta and the blue dragon.

Tony's head was spinning and aching at

the same time. All he knew was that somebody was so worried about what Lady Greensleeves saw that he or she got the woman out of the neighborhood.

"Mama," Tony said that night, "I'm pretty sure it was a blue car that hit Soroya."

Mrs. Gibbs set a steaming pot of stew on the table and began ladling out portions. "Lots of blue cars in the world," she remarked.

"Well, if I see a blue car with front-end damage, Mama, I'm gonna look real close," Tony said.

"Tony, just forget about that accident, will you?" Mrs. Gibbs said, sounding exasperated. "Whoever hit that poor child didn't mean to do it. It was an accident. Lord, we all do bad things, and sometimes we don't have the courage to own up to what we done. What if you find some poor weak fool who hit her and then took off like a scared rabbit? Is that gonna make the child heal faster?"

"You think they should get away with what they did?" Tony demanded. "That's not justice!"

Mrs. Gibbs gave a bitter laugh. "You

think there's justice in this world? You got a thing or two to learn, boy. Plenty folks gettin' away with murder. Then some poor hungry mother steals a couple a cans of baby food and she's hauled before the judge. And meanwhile, you got these bankers thievin' away millions and nobody blinks an eye. Wake up, boy. Mind your own business and let things be."

"You didn't want me to look for who killed Mr. Jefferson either, Mama. But I did and I'm glad!" Tony said.

"Yeah, but that was different. Whoever did this is trembling in their shoes, and they're gonna know all their lives what they did. That's punishment enough. Now eat your stew before it gets cold. Lord, it's bad enough warm without eating it cold," Mrs. Gibbs said.

Tony ate in silence. But he resolved to keep his eyes peeled for a blue car with the kind of damage caused by hitting somebody. He figured he might just get lucky.

* * *

At track and field practice on Friday afternoon, Coach Shaw was all excited.

The Adams Bobcats were running in competition with the Lincoln Lances the next day. And the coach was determined this would be the start of the march to the championship.

"You and Zenza Dunne are gonna do it for us in the relay," the coach thundered at Tony. "You're a great finisher, Tony. So when Zenza hands you the baton, I'm pretty sure it's going to depend on you to bring in the numbers."

Zenza laughed. "Gonna depend on him? Man, we're dead roaches."

The coach didn't smile. He put great stock in team loyalty. Now he glowered at Zenza and said, "You'll be doing some extra push-ups for that crack, Dunne!"

Zenza walked off, muttering to himself. Tony sometimes wondered why Zenza was even on the team at all. He didn't seem to care much about anything or anybody. So how come he was so interested in running?

Tony shrugged. He guessed that even guys like Zenza had to have something to live for. And Zenza was a good runner. Not that Tony himself was in the mood for running lately.

"I'm not feeling so good about the meet tomorrow," Tony told the coach.

"You're not gonna let us all down, are you, Gibbs?" Coach Shaw stared hard at Tony. "Because if you are, then you're not made of the kind of stuff I thought you were. If you're the kind that chickens out in a crunch, then I don't hold much hope for your future, Gibbs!"

"Okay, okay," Tony muttered. "I'll do the best I can."

It was almost dark when practice was over. Though his legs felt like lead weights, Tony began searching the neighborhood for a damaged blue car.

As Tony walked the streets, he spotted a yellow four-door with a punched-in back fender and a couple of black pickups with various dents. There were a lot of red cars but not that many blue ones. There were black and beige and silver cars. And he saw a lot of junkers covered with dirt and rust. He couldn't even tell what color they used to be.

Then, as Tony was about to head for home, he spotted a blue import. It was parked in the back of the store that used to belong to Mr. Jefferson. It was a fancy, shiny car—a shiny blue dragon? Tony squinted. But he was too far away to tell if there was any damage on the front.

Tony sprinted toward the car. His pulse raced at the thought that this might be it. Maybe the car belonged to the rich absentee owner of the grocery store. Without doubt, he was a guy who'd be rich enough to spirit Lady Greensleeves away.

"Hey, punk!" came a sharp voice just behind Tony. He turned in surprise, and a burly man grabbed him. Tony tried to wrestle free, but another muscular man joined in. They shoved Tony down to the blacktop, banging his face on the rough surface of the parking lot.

8 "TRYING TO STEAL some wheels for yourself, punk?" the first man asked.

"No," Tony gasped. He felt his lip bleeding. "I'm just admiring the car."

The first man laughed. "Yeah sure, kid."

"You're all dirty little thieves," added the second man. "How come you don't try working for a living, eh? Eh?" And they banged Tony's face into the blacktop again.

"You show your face around this parking lot again and you'll end up with a broken neck. Got it?" the first man snarled. "Now get up and beat it while you're still breathing."

Tony struggled to his feet, his face burning with shame. His insides churned with resentment. He'd gotten close enough to the car to get a good look at it. Close enough to see that there wasn't a scratch on it.

Tony had suffered all this pain and

humiliation for nothing! He felt a wild, almost choking hatred for the pair who laughed as he ran off.

Tony was just about home when he heard a car horn. Turning, he saw Lew Shaw leaning his head out of a beat-up old car.

"Need a ride, Tony?" the coach called out. He pulled to a stop at the curb.

Tony waved. He opened his mouth to answer, "No, thanks," when suddenly he stopped. Tony's head began ringing. His breathing tightened and he almost felt like he was being smothered.

Tony stared at Coach Shaw's car in stunned disbelief. Under the streetlight, he saw that the car was a faded blue. And the front fender was bent all out of shape.

Tony's head continued ringing. He wondered if he was going to faint. Finally he was able to get some words out. "Thanks," he gasped. "But I live right there." He pointed to his building.

"Okay," said Coach Shaw. Then he peered closer at Tony's bloodied face. "You been in a fight or what? Real smart to get banged up the night before a big race."

"I fell down," Tony lied. Then he asked, "You live around here?"

"Couple of blocks away," Coach replied. "But I've got some friends on this street."

Tony was shaking so hard he felt his teeth chattering. What was he supposed to do? How could he say, "By the way, Coach, did you happen to run my girl down on Monday night?"

The coach's voice broke into Tony's thoughts. "You all right, Gibbs? You don't look too well."

"I'm fine," Tony answered. His voice wasn't much louder than a whisper. But he couldn't let the coach go yet. He had to find out if his suspicions were true.

"What happened to your car?" Tony asked, motioning toward the bent fender.

"Oh, that," Coach Shaw said with a little laugh. "It was like that when I bought it. This baby may not be beautiful, but she gets me where I want to go."

Tony looked into Lew Shaw's eyes, trying to decide if he was telling the truth.

"Oh," was all Tony could say.

"Well," said Coach, "go home and get some sleep. You've got a big race tomorrow.

And get that face taken care of," he added. With a wave, he drove off.

Tony walked home in a daze. No, no, no, he thought to himself. Coach Shaw wasn't that kind of person. Granted, Tony admitted, the coach did get on his nerves sometimes. But no way would he hit a person and then drive off.

And yet...Tony couldn't shake the fact that Lew Shaw's car was blue. And it did have front-end damage. He entered his apartment, feeling sick. But as much as his face hurt, his heart hurt a hundred times worse.

"You what?" Mrs. Gibbs exclaimed when Tony told her what happened to him.

"I was looking at a blue car behind Mr. Jefferson's old store when these guys jumped me," Tony said.

"Good Lord, boy!" his mother wailed. "Don't you know they got security men at night to keep cars from getting stolen all through that strip mall? What you think those men gonna think when they see a boy like you messing around the cars? You're lucky to be here with a busted lip and a few scratches 'stead of blown away!"

Shauna stood in her bathrobe in the kitchen doorway. "Was it the right car, Tony?" she asked.

"Don't be feeding his craziness, girl," Mrs. Gibbs snapped. She dabbed at Tony's face with a disinfectant. "Right car, wrong car, don't matter!"

"Wasn't the right car," Tony said stubbornly. "But the right car is out there somewhere. And I'm gonna find it." He forced himself not to think of Lew Shaw.

But that night in bed, Tony lay awake for a long time. Did Coach Shaw do it or didn't he? And if he did, how could Tony prove it? Did he even want to prove it? Tony's head swam with all the questions.

He turned his thoughts to the men who had jumped him. How could those men—those strangers—treat him like that just because of how he looked? How could they get away with doing that? And what could he do about it?

Nothing. And that's what tore at him. Somebody could run Soroya down and get away with it. Some rich person who could afford to steal a witness. Some rich guy who could hire hoods to beat Tony up for just looking at a car.

And that made Tony think of something else. Surely Lew Shaw couldn't have hired some guy with a Cadillac to spirit away a witness. Teachers and coaches at Adams didn't make much money. Unless the guy with the Caddy was a friend of the coach.

Tony restlessly tossed and turned. He didn't figure he could take much more without exploding.

The next day at the track, Coach Shaw glared at Tony. "I hope your legs are better than your looks today," the coach said. "Otherwise, the Lincoln Lances will make hamburger out of us."

Tony felt like punching somebody, any-body. He hoped the coach got off his case real quick or he'd end up throwing a punch at him. If Tony got mad enough, he might even accuse Coach Shaw of being the hit-and-run driver. And Tony didn't want to do that—not yet.

"Back off, coach," Tony said savagely.

Coach Shaw did a double take when he saw the rage in the boy's eyes. He didn't say anything for a minute. Then he com-mented softly, "You look like I musta looked that time in boarding school when I got punished for speaking my own language. Something like that happen to you, Gibbs?"

"Something like that happened, yeah," Tony said. He was surprised by the coach's insight.

"Put it in the race, Tony," Coach Shaw urged him. "Winning is the best revenge. Put all the fury in the race. That's what I did. Run the rage out of you."

Soon Tony's relay was announced. The gun popped, and Kirby Hacker took off. He ran a good first lap for the Bobcats. But when he passed the baton to Chad, the team was already several seconds behind the Lances.

Chad looked desperate as he grabbed the baton and sprinted down the course. But in spite of his best efforts, the Bobcats still lagged when Chad passed the baton to Zenza. Zenza became a blur, traveling at a pounding pace. When he passed the baton to Tony, the teams were dead even.

It was Tony's race to win or lose. A glint in Zenza's eyes said to Tony, "Go on. Give it to the Lincoln Lances. Then everybody will know you for the nothin' you are!"

9 TONY GRABBED THE baton and sped on, demanding every ounce of strength he had. Each time he hit the ground, he felt it was a blow struck against the driver who hit Soroya. It was a pounding against the men who beat and humiliated him when he'd done nothing wrong.

Tony ran his rage into the dust of the track, just like Coach Shaw told him to do. He let the hatred flow through his body like high octane gas in a sports car. Then he forced it out of himself like exhaust fumes.

Faster and faster Tony strode. He put himself completely into the race and out of himself. When he crossed the finish line, he didn't even know what the screaming and cheering was all about.

The Adams Bobcats had beaten the Lances in record time. It was one for the books.

Coach Shaw whooped as he ran to the

team. He hugged Tony and the other relay runners, yelling his lungs out. Even Zenza said, "Aw-right, Gibbs!"

Shauna leaped into Tony's arms. For just a few seconds Tony felt like he did in the old days after a good race. He was happy. But then he remembered Soroya wasn't there, just like Mr. Jefferson wasn't there. The joy drained out of his heart like water from a shattered glass.

* * *

At school on Monday, Tony saw Mr. Campbell shouting in the faculty parking lot. Ms. Cheng was with him. She was speaking to him in a low voice, trying to calm him down. It was an incredible scene.

"Somebody keyed my car. Look at it!" Mr. Campbell cried. He seemed near hysteria. "My car is ruined!"

"I'm sure it can be fixed, Mr. Campbell," Ms. Cheng said. "Your insurance will pay for it."

"Of course the insurance will pay," Mr. Campbell raved. "But it'll never get fixed right! They never get the finish right after something like this."

The angry teacher threw his briefcase to the ground. "Man, oh man, I stayed around here too long. Brittany is right. This is just a jungle full of wild animals!"

"Please, Mr. Campbell, get a hold of yourself," Ms. Cheng said.

"Heyyy, Mistuh Campbell," Wayman sneered, "somebody done messed up your pretty machine. You got enemies or what?"

Mr. Campbell glared fiercely at Wayman. Tony knew Wayman had flunked the last American Democracy test. Was that why this had happened? But Mr. Campbell'd flunked several students on the last test. Any one of them—or none of them—could be the culprit.

Tony shook his head when he saw the damaged car. "Too bad, Mr. Campbell."

"Savage, mindless vandalism," Mr. Campbell stormed.

Tony wondered why Mr. Campbell brought such expensive wheels into a neighborhood where most people had nothing.

Tony looked sadly at his teacher. Soroya probably meant less to Mr. Campbell than a scratch on his car. Tony wanted to be a success some day. But he never wanted to be like Mr. Campbell. He never wanted things to become more important than people.

That night Tony received a call from Denique.

"Tony!" she said excitedly, "Soroya moved just a tiny bit. A nurse said her legs moved."

"Man—that's terrific! I'll be over there right after school tomorrow," Tony said, a big grin on his face.

"Who just elected you president?" Tony's mother asked when he'd hung up. "You look on top of the world."

"Mama, Denique said Soroya moved a little—that's a good sign. Means maybe she's coming out of the coma soon. You hear me, Mama?" Tony hugged his mother and danced her around the kitchen floor.

"Well, thank the Lord she's better," Mrs. Gibbs said. "Lots of us been prayin'. Especially Shauna. That child has the kind of faith that could move the Rocky Mountains to downtown L.A.!"

Outside the school the next morning, Michelle said, "Well, I'm glad she's moving a little. But that doesn't necessarily mean she's going to be normal, Tony. You better not get your hopes up too high. Maybe it sounds romantic to think of loving some poor helpless brain-damaged girl. But that gets old mighty fast when she's dragging you down."

"Girl, I need you like I need a bath in a dumpster," Tony snapped.

"Okay, yell at me if it makes you feel better, Tony. But I know the kind of stories my aunt tells me from the nursing home," Michelle said.

"Hey, look," Zenza shouted. "Old Campbell is wheeling up in a Lincoln—a shiny black Lincoln Town Car."

They drifted over to the parking lot to see Mr. Campbell getting out with his briefcase. He glared at the assembled grinning faces and said, "Don't even think about messing with this car. Anybody who touches this car can depend on a lifetime suspension from the school system of this city! Come within ten yards of this car with a key, and you'll wish you were dead! This car belongs to Ms. Austin."

"Ooooo," Wayman whispered mockingly.

"It belongs to Miss Britt-an-y. Lordy, if her pretty car gets keyed, she's gonna whip Mr. Campbell's backside with a wet noodle!"

Laughter exploded. Mr. Campbell strode forward, his eyes ablaze. "I'm not kidding. Anybody who goes near that car is dead meat!"

"Wow, this is serious business. We all best be shakin' in our socks," Wayman snickered.

Mr. Campbell stomped past, cursing under his breath.

"Where's Mr. Campbell's car?" Michelle asked.

"Getting fixed, I guess," Andre said. "Getting the scratch taken out."

"Where's that girl get off havin' a Lincoln Town Car anyway?" Michelle said, envy gleaming in her eyes. "What is she, maybe twenty-four years old at most?"

"Don't you know, girl?" Andre replied. "Her daddy owns a big computer business. He prob'ly buys her a new Lincoln every time she has a birthday."

The day dragged by slowly for Tony. He could hardly wait to get to the hospital. Maybe Soroya will be awake when I get there, Tony thought. Maybe she'll grin at me and say, "Well, it's about time you got here!"

Finally the last bell rang. Twenty minutes later, Tony climbed off the bus in front of the hospital. He hurried into the lobby and waited impatiently for the elevator. His heart pounded in anticipation as he raced down the hall to room 312.

"Hi, Tony," Denique said when he came in.

Tony entered the room slowly. He was immediately crushed with disappointment. Soroya didn't look any different. She was still as motionless as ever.

Tony's heart sank. Maybe the nurse who saw her move had just been imagining things.

"They say she's improving, but I don't see it," Denique said.

"Yeah," Tony agreed. He stepped to Soroya's side and gently stroked her forehead. "Baby, can you hear me?" he said softly. "Remember when I kissed you and you giggled and I was insulted? I said, 'You mean I kiss funny?' And you said I kiss just fine and you always giggle when you're happy."

He paused, then said, "Everybody's missing you at school. School…baby, you wouldn't believe what's happening at school. Somebody keyed Mr. Campbell's car and he flipped. Now he's driving Ms. Brittany Austin's Lincoln."

Soroya didn't seem to hear any of Tony's monologue. She remained still. But Denique remarked, "I know Brit Austin. She was in my psych class in college. Boy, is she rich. Everybody envied her. We'd come to school all packed in a little VW, and she'd come tooling up in her very own baby blue Lincoln."

"She's got a black Lincoln now," Tony said.

Denique shrugged. "I guess she's got a different one now."

Tony felt a chill crawl up his spine. A blue Lincoln? A "shiny blue dragon"? No, it was crazy. Brittany Austin driving down Central that night? Why? She hated this neighborhood enough during the day. She wouldn't come within a hundred miles of it at night.

And yet…it was still a possibility. What

if she hit Soroya in that big car and just raced on? What if she got the dents taken out of the front end and got the car repainted black? What if she was the one who hired that man to come take Lady Greensleeves away?

Now that Tony thought about it, she had heard him talking to Mr. Campbell about Lady Greensleeves being a witness. He hadn't thought anything of it at the time. But now he recalled that she had rushed out in an awful hurry.

Tony could think of nothing else as he went down to the hospital lobby to a phone. He flipped through the phone book until he found her name. No address was listed, but there it was: B. Austin. Lots of women listed themselves that way so guys wouldn't know it was a woman's number.

Tony hit the buttons with trembling fingers and waited for what seemed like forever. Then her crisp voice came on the line. "Hello?"

"Is this Ms. Austin?" Tony asked. He had a very deep voice. So it was no problem pretending he was a man instead of a boy.

"Yes, who's this?" she snapped. She

sounded impatient. She was always in a hurry. Maybe that night on Central she was in such a hurry she never saw the girl in the yellow raincoat—or saw her too late.

"Ma'am, I work at the body shop where you got your Lincoln fixed and painted. We found a coin purse on the floor in the office. We're calling customers who were in here recently, asking if the purse belongs to them."

There was a long silence. Then she said, "I didn't lose any coin purse."

"Ma'am," Tony said, "we noticed you seemed real nervous when you brought the car in. Is everything okay?"

"What is this? Who are you?" Brittany Austin's voice became high-pitched. "Are you some greasy little creep who thinks he can blackmail me or something? Well, you won't get away with it!"

10 TONY TRIED TO keep his voice even. "Ma'am," he said, "we just want to return the coin purse."

The phone banged in Tony's ear. Tony stood there shaking so hard he almost dropped the phone. She sounded terrified of blackmail. That meant she'd done something, didn't it?

Tony felt a pounding in his head. He knew—he just knew—that he was close to solving the mystery. Now he just had to figure out a way to prove his suspicions.

The next morning, Tony waited for Mr. Campbell in the faculty parking lot. He still hadn't fully gotten over the shakes at what he thought he'd discovered. When Mr. Campbell pulled up in the Lincoln, Tony rushed to the car before the teacher had even turned off the engine.

"I gotta talk to you, Mr. Campbell—it's real important," Tony said.

"All right, let me get out of the car, will

you?" Mr. Campbell said. Then, once out, he asked, "What's up?"

Tony blurted out his suspicions. "I think this Lincoln did the hit-and-run on Soroya."

"What?" Mr. Campbell gasped. "Are you crazy, Tony? Ms. Austin's car? That's the most ridiculous thing I've ever heard."

"An old lady saw the accident. Remember I told you about Lady Greensleeves? She talked about a blue dragon, and I figure that means a blue car. This Lincoln used to be blue, and it had front-end damage," Tony said.

"Cool down, Gibbs. You're talking non-sense," Mr. Campbell said. However, a wary look was creeping into the teacher's eyes. "It so happens that Brittany did have a minor accident a short time ago. She told me it happened in a parking lot. And since the car needed to be in the shop anyway, she decided to have it painted black. She said she always preferred that color."

"I'd like to know what body shop did the work. If you don't know, will you ask her for me?" Tony requested.

"Now wait a minute. Where do you get off asking me these kinds of questions, as if you're the law! I don't have to stand for this."

Mr. Campbell paused. Then he said, "Besides, Ms. Austin's business is no longer mine."

Tony stared. "What do you mean by that?"

Mr. Campbell seemed embarrassed. "There's no need to broadcast this. But after tonight, Ms. Austin and I will no longer be engaged."

"No longer engaged!" Tony exclaimed. "What—?"

"Never mind," Mr. Campbell interrupted. "Now, I have a class to meet, so please excuse me." The teacher brushed past Tony, his face like steel.

It wasn't like Tony to cut classes. But this morning was different. He sprinted from the school grounds directly to the police station.

There he told an officer that he thought a black Lincoln parked at Adams might have been involved in the Curtis hit-and-run. He gave the officer the license number. The officer promised he'd look into it.

Tony went home then. He just couldn't handle school today with his insides churning like a washing machine. The apartment was empty, so he cleaned it up. He even started dinner before his mother came home.

"What're you doing home?" Mrs. Gibbs asked when she walked in the door that afternoon.

"I didn't feel so well this morning, Mama. But I started feeling better, so I did some cleaning and cooking. Thought you needed a rest," Tony said.

Mrs. Gibbs stared at her son curiously. "Well, I appreciate it. But you sure there's not more to this? You keeping your nose clean?"

"Yes, Mama," Tony said.

"Well, then, you just let me take over the dinner now," his mother said. "I suppose I'll have to write you a note for tomorrow."

The next day at school, Andre rushed up to Tony. "You shoulda been here yesterday afternoon, man," he said. "Cops came to look the Lincoln over. They were crawling around and peeking underneath. Then they called for a tow truck and away it went."

Overhearing Andre, Zenza laughed. "Maybe that car is hot. Maybe Ms. Brittany boots cars!"

"I think the Lincoln hit Soroya," Tony said.

"You're kidding, man!" Andre gasped. "Mr. Campbell?"

Tony shook his head. "Ms. Austin, I figure. The car had front-end damage, and it's just been painted."

"Wow!" Andre exclaimed in wonderment. "Ms. Brittany Austin in trouble with the law. I can't believe it! I wonder what Campbell thinks?"

"Somehow I don't think he'll really care," Tony replied.

"What do you mean?" asked Andre.

Tony told him about his conversation with Mr. Campbell.

"Sounds like Campbell finally got smart," Andre remarked. "But what about that job he had with her father's company?"

"Hey, I forgot about that," said Tony. "I bet those big bucks he was counting on next year won't be rollin' in after all."

By afternoon the police had determined that Brittany Austin's car was indeed the car involved in the hit-and-run. The car parts taken from the accident scene matched the Lincoln.

Apparently Ms. Austin hadn't taken her broken engagement very well. She told the police she hadn't been using the car that night. She had loaned it to Bruce Campbell. The only problem with that was that twelve teachers had seen him at a faculty meeting at the time Soroya was struck. When Brittany heard this, she finally broke down and admitted to hitting Soroya. In fact, she'd been on her way to pick up Mr. Campbell when the accident occurred.

"So she did it," Tony bitterly said to Andre. "That rich girl came over here and ran Soroya down and didn't even stop. I'd stop if I hit a dog. But she didn't even stop to see if Soroya needed help."

Tony thought he'd feel elated about tracking down the hit-and-run driver. Instead, he just felt tired and sad. Every day he made his way to the hospital and nothing ever changed. But still he went.

In midweek Tony told Soroya about Ms. Austin being arrested. He told her about how he helped the Bobcats win another relay. Then Tony bent down and kissed the silent girl good-bye. "See you tomorrow, baby," he whispered.

As Tony stepped out into the dark street outside the hospital, he nearly bumped into Brittany Austin.

"What're you doing here?" he asked her. "Why aren't you in jail?"

"In jail? Not while my father has a dime for bail! Do you actually think I'll go to jail for some stupid accident? That little fool stepped out in front of me. It wasn't even my fault. And as for why I didn't stop—in that neighborhood? Are you kidding?"

Tony stared at her in disgust. "That's why you followed me here—to tell me that?"

"No. I wanted you to know that your stupid little detective game probably ruined my life. My relationship with Bruce is over," she said.

"Oh, really?" Tony almost told her what he knew—how Mr. Campbell was ready to break off the engagement even before her arrest. But he decided to keep quiet. After all, what good would it do?

"Sneer at me all you like, you little punk," Ms. Austin said. "But you've caused me a lot of grief, and I'm going to make you pay for it. You've ruined my future, and I'm going to ruin yours!"

Without answering, Tony walked past the woman and then sprinted for home. He thought he'd feel more hatred for her, but he didn't. She was almost pathetic.

The next afternoon, when Tony arrived for track practice, the coach took him into his private office. He closed the door after them.

"You look real serious, Coach," Tony remarked. "What's up?" Tony found it hard to look at the coach in the face. He felt guilty about his earlier suspicions of him.

"I got a phone call last night that I want you to know about," Coach Shaw said. "It was from a pretty big man. The man said he was planning to donate a lot of money to the athletic program here at Adams. Lord knows we could use the money.

"But," Coach Shaw continued, "he was hesitant to do that. It seems he has a real concern about the moral character of one of our athletes. He said this dude Tony

Gibbs is dealing crack."

"That's a lie," Tony snapped.

"I figured as much. But I wanted to hear it from you. Now, the big man wants you dumped from the track team. Otherwise, no new equipment, no new uniforms... nothing."

"Tell me something, Coach. Was the big man's name Austin?" Tony asked.

His coach's face broke into a grin. "Are you psychic or something, Gibbs?"

"Yeah, well, I found the goods on his daughter, and she said she'd get even. I guess she got her daddy to do the dirty work," Tony said.

"Well, if we keep you on the team, we stand to lose a lot of stuff, Gibbs," Coach Shaw said.

"It's your call, Coach," Tony said.

"Yeah...no new volleyballs, no new nets, no new jackets, no new lights. But we get to keep the best damn sprinter this town has ever produced. And something else too, Gibbs. We get to keep our integrity. Now what do you think my call will be?" Coach Shaw asked. His eyes sparkled with humor.

Tony grinned. "I guess we keep on going for the championship, huh?"

"You got it, Tony." Coach Shaw slapped Tony on the back. Just then Ms. Cheng, the principal, knocked and walked in.

"Mr. Shaw," she said. "I've got some news about that phone call of yours. Frankly, I found it hard to believe that Gerald Austin would do such a thing. He and his wife are good friends of mine. I just couldn't imagine either of them acting in such a way.

"So I called Gerald myself," Ms. Cheng went on. "And, just as I thought, he insisted that he never called you. In fact, he couldn't understand why anyone would impersonate him. I mentioned to him what this caller said to you about a donation. So Gerald decided on the spot to make a very generous donation to Adams High himself!"

Coach Shaw laughed out loud. "Well, all right! This school could really use it."

"Yeah," said Tony. "That's the best news I've heard in a long time." Now if only there'd be some good news about Soroya, he thought.

Tony was feeling more and more desperate about Soroya. It became harder every day to make himself believe Soroya would ever wake up. But still he had to keep going and keep hoping.

After track practice, Tony headed out as usual to see Soroya. In her hospital room, he pulled up a chair and took the sleeping girl's hand. Taking a deep breath, he began to talk to her.

"Come on, baby," Tony urged. "Open those beautiful eyes. Please, Soroya, I miss you so much. Everybody misses—"

"Tony!" Mrs. Curtis gasped. "She blinked! Did you see that? Oh my God, don't let it be my imagination!"

Tony continued talking in a louder voice, "Soroya, we're here for you, babe. Come on, open your eyes—you can do it."

"Oh my God, look, look!" Mrs. Curtis cried. Soroya's eyes were flickering open and shut. Tony grabbed her hands.

"Baby, baby, do you hear me? Do you hear me? I love you, baby!" Tony cried.

"Love ya," Soroya whispered back. Then she was off again, asleep. Tony and Mrs. Curtis hugged each other and screamed so loud that the nurses came running.

For the next few days Soroya was in and out of consciousness. Yet each day showed some improvement. The doctor said that there was every reason to believe she'd have a full recovery.

Tony visited Soroya daily. One windy day he brought news from the courthouse. "Well, it seems Brittany had some trouble convincing the court to dismiss her case. The lady who hit you has to do some jail time and community service."

"I'm not mad at her," Soroya told Tony. "I'm just sad it happened. I was in the intersection, and I know I had the light."

Tony thought again of what Soroya had said a while back: "Death loves a shining mark." He felt a rush of love for Soroya. He gave her a big hug and thought, I'm not letting go of this shining mark for a long time.

The door to the room opened then. Tony looked up, and his eyes widened. "Mr. Campbell!"

Mr. Campbell refused to meet Tony's eyes. "I just came to see how Soroya's doing," he said.

"Much better, Mr. Campbell," Soroya said

with a smile. "But I'm feeling real cooped up here. I can't wait to get back to school!"

"Well, we can't wait to have you back," said Mr. Campbell. "And speaking of school..." He finally looked at Tony. "I guess I'll be back at Adams next year after all."

"Lost your computer job, huh," Tony said.

"Actually, Ms. Austin's father told me the job is mine if I want it. But I turned it down. I guess I never realized before just how much I enjoy teaching. Sure, it's got its share of problems. But I've got a responsibility to all you kids. I want to be around to make sure your dreams don't die."

Soroya smiled again. "I've always said anything can happen if you keep on dreaming." Tony put his arms around Soroya. He thought about his dream of making it to the Olympics. Tony felt that if he ran a race right now, he'd have enough strength to sprint to the clouds, straight through the halo of the moon.

"Soroya," said Tony, "just promise me one thing. Do your dreaming with your eyes wide open. You've done enough sleeping for a while!"

PASSAGES novels
by Anne Schraff